Baby Grizzly

By Beth Spanjian
Illustrated by John Butler

MERRIGOLD PRESS • NEW YORK

Text © 1988 Angel Entertainment, Inc. Illustrations © 1988 John Butler. All rights reserved. First published by Longmeadow Press. Printed in the U.S.A. No part of this book may be reproduced or copied in any form without written permission from the publisher. All trademarks are the property of Merrigold Press, Racine, Wisconsin 53402. Library of Congress Catalog Card Number 90-81284 ISBN 0-307-10904-6   MCMXCIV

Baby Grizzly is sound asleep
with her little brown nose buried
in her mother's warm, fuzzy belly.
It is a cool summer morning.

Suddenly, a playful ball of fur
pounces on top of Baby Grizzly.
It is her twin brother,
telling her it is time to get up!

The two young bear cubs wrestle and play,
while their mother digs up tasty roots
and bulbs with her powerful paws.

After their romp, the cubs settle down
to rest on a patch of cool grass. When Mother
Grizzly has finished digging for breakfast,
she comes and licks Baby Grizzly clean.

Suddenly, Mother Grizzly rears up on her
hind legs to sniff the air. Humans are near.
They are campers who have come to the woods for
a vacation. Mother Grizzly wants her family to be
left alone. She hurries her young ones away.

The bears find a clear mountain stream. Brightly colored fish dart through the cool water. Mother Grizzly spends the afternoon catching the tasty fish for lunch. Baby Grizzly and her brother are in for a treat!

Baby Grizzly tries to catch a fish, too,
but she makes a big splash
and scares all the fish away!

Dripping wet, Mother Grizzly joins her cubs on the grass beside the stream. The ground seems to rock when Mother Grizzly shakes herself dry. Baby Grizzly learns how to take care of herself from her mother. She shakes herself dry, too.

The three grizzlies find a soft, comfortable
spot for their afternoon nap.
The cubs are hungry for their mother's
warm milk.

Soon, evening comes to the backcountry.
The bears hear thunder rumbling
off the mountains, and smell
the clean summer rain.

When the sky is dark, and the moon shines
down through the trees, the three bears nestle
together on a bed of dry pine needles.
Then they all fall fast asleep.

Facts About Baby Grizzly

Where Do Grizzlies Live?

Grizzlies live in parts of Idaho, Montana, Wyoming and Washington. They feed in open meadows, but sleep and find shelter in forests. Around October, the bears dig cozy dens and sleep there without eating or drinking until they awake in spring. This is called "hibernation." Hundreds of thousands of grizzlies once roamed throughout most of the western United States. Today, fewer than one thousand grizzlies exist in the continental United States.

What Do Grizzlies Eat?

Grizzlies eat mostly plants and grasses. They have long, curved front claws for digging up bulbs and grubs. Grizzlies also eat fish, berries, pine nuts, rodents and other animals, especially those that are weak from the long winter months. All summer and fall, the bears eat to their hearts' content, building up thick layers of fat. In the winter, during hibernation, a grizzly's body temperature drops and its heart rate and breathing slow way down. Their fat keeps them warm and gives them the energy they need to survive the winter.

How Do Grizzlies Communicate?

Grizzlies talk to each other with body language. The way they move their head, mouth and ears—even the way they walk—means a lot to another grizzly. They also communicate with growls, roars and other sounds.

How Big Are Grizzlies, and How Long Do They Live?

When cubs are born, they are only a foot long and weigh less than two pounds. By the time they leave their den, they have grown to ten pounds. Adult females (called sows) and adult males (called boars) can weigh anywhere from two hundred to one thousand pounds! Grizzlies can live up to twenty-five years in the wild. The oldest grizzly in a zoo lived to be thirty-five years old.

What Is a Grizzly's Family Like?

Sows usually have two cubs per litter. Some sows have as many as four. A mother grizzly breeds in June and July. She gives birth to her cubs in late January or early February, while in her den. The cubs don't know who their father is, for he doesn't help raise them. The mother cares for her cubs until they are two or three years old and go off on their own.

What Is the Grizzly's Future?

Because so few grizzlies exist in the continental United States, they are called a "threatened" species. Grizzlies are getting special attention, since they could become extinct without help from wildlife managers. To survive, the bears need large, remote areas where they won't bother people, and people won't bother them. The key to the grizzly's survival is teaching people how to respect the bears and live with them in peace.